First published by Parragon in 2012
Parragon
Chartist House
15–17 Trim Street
Bath BA1 1HA, UK
www.parragon.com

Edited by: Gemma Louise Lowe
Designed by: Jim Willmott
Production by: Jack Aylward

ISBN 978-1-78186-048-9

Printed in China

101 DALMATIANS

PaRragon

Bath · New York · Singapore · Hong Kong · Cologne · Delhi
Melbourne · Amsterdam · Johannesburg · Shenzhen

Roger Radcliff was a musician. He lived in a little house in London with Pongo, his pet Dalmatian.

One day, Roger got married. His lovely new wife was named Anita—and she had a beautiful lady Dalmatian named Perdita.

Soon, Perdita was expecting her first litter of puppies. Life seemed perfect until one day, an old friend of Anita's, Cruella De Vil, came to visit. Perita and Pongo were frightened of her.

"Where are the puppies?" Cruella demanded.

"They're not expected for another three weeks," Anita replied.

"You must let me know when they arrive. I just adore Dalmatian puppies—their coats are so beautiful." And with that, Cruella swept out of the house in a flurry.

Three weeks later, Perdita and Pongo
became the proud parents of fifteen puppies.
Roger, Anita and Nanny, the housekeeper,
were delighted.

The very next day, Cruella returned. "Fifteen puppies!" she cried, excitedly. "I'll buy all of them."

"Oh no, you won't," said Roger. "They're not for sale."

"You fools! You'll be sorry!" Cruella cried, storming out of the house.

One night soon after, Cruella's henchmen, Horace and Jasper Badun, lay in wait to dognap the puppies. They sat in their van and waited for Roger and Anita to take Perdita and Pongo for their evening walk.

Once the coast was clear, the Baduns forced their way into the house. When Nanny tried to stop them, the Baduns locked her in a broom closet.

By the time Nanny managed to escape, the Baduns were gone—and so were the puppies!

The police immediately launched an investigation, but as the days went by, the puppies were still not found.

At last, Pongo said to Perdita, "The humans aren't getting anywhere. We'll have to find the puppies ourselves."

Pongo decided to try the Twilight Bark. This was the quickest way for dogs to send and receive news across the country.

That evening, when the two Dalmatians were taken for their walk, Pongo barked the alert—three loud barks and a howl—from the top of Primrose Hill.

After a moment an answering bark was heard. "It's the Great Dane at Hampstead!" Pongo said to Perdita, and he barked out his message.

Danny the Great Dane was very surprised by the message. "Fifteen Dalmatian puppies have been stolen!" he told a terrier friend. "The humans haven't been able to find them, so it's up to us to send out an all-dog alert with the Twilight Bark."

Danny's big deep voice began to send the news all over London . . .

Two mongrels heard the alert. One said, "I think we should let the rest of the country know."

And so, within the hour, word had spread north, south, east, and west—all over England.

Before too long, the Twilight Bark reached an old sheepdog named Colonel, who lived on a farm.

Colonel's friends—a horse named Captain and a cat named Tibs—listened too. They were all very surprised to hear that fifteen puppies had been stolen!

"That's funny," Tibs said to Captain and Colonel.
"I heard puppies barking over at the old De Vil house
last night."

"But no one lives there now," said Colonel.

"We must go and see what's going on."

So Colonel and Tibs went quietly up to the house and peered through a broken window.

Inside the house, Horace and Jasper Badun were eating supper and relaxing in front of the television.

All around the room there were puppies. Not fifteen—nor even fifty—but ninety-nine of them!

Colonel quickly returned to Captain's stable and loudly barked the good news. Within no time at all, the Twilight Bark sent the message all the way back to London that the puppies had been found.

It finally reached the ears of Perdita and Pongo. They set off across the snowy countryside as fast as they could to rescue their puppies.

Meanwhile, Sergeant Tibs was keeping watch on the house. When he saw Cruella drive up to the front door, he went to the broken window to hear what was happening.

Cruella was ordering the Baduns to kill the puppies! "I want their skins for fur coats!" she cried. "I'll be back first thing in the morning." And with that warning hanging in the air, she turned and was gone.

Tibs was horrified. Fur coats from puppy skins! What a terrible thought.

There wasn't a moment to lose. As soon as the Baduns began watching television again, Tibs crept through the broken window and whispered to the nearest puppy, "Tell everyone they must escape. Cruella is after your coats!"

When all the puppies had been
alerted, Tibs led them to a hiding
place.

As soon as the Baduns discovered that the puppies had gone, they searched all over the house and eventually found them cowering under the stairs. Tibs was in front, ready to protect them from the Baduns.

Meanwhile, Colonel had met up with Perdita and Pongo and led them to the De Vil house. They arrived just in the nick of time and quickly bounded into action.

Perdita attacked Horace Badun, while Pongo tore at Jasper Badun's trousers.

Under cover of the fight, Tibs led the puppies out of the house to the safety of Captain's stable.

Leaving the Baduns in a heap
on the floor, Perdita and Pongo,
dashed after the puppies.

"Are our fifteen all here?"
asked Perdita anxiously.

"Your fifteen and a few more"
replied Captain. "There are
ninety-nine!"

"Ninety-nine!" said Pongo, astonished. "Whatever did Cruella want with ninety-nine puppies?"

There was silence for a moment, then one little puppy said, "She was going to make fur coats out of us."

Perdita and Pongo looked at each other in horror. They had never heard of anything so evil.

"We'll just have to take them all back to London with us," said Perdita. "I'm sure Roger and Anita will look after them."

Perdita, Pongo and the puppies set off back to London, leaving a trail of paw prints in the snow.

Cruella, who had returned for the puppies' coats, quickly spotted the paw prints, and the chase began!

Eventually, after trudging across the cold countryside, Perdita and Pongo led the tired puppies to the shelter of a blacksmith's shop. Cruella and the Baduns were still on their trail, determined to catch them.

Suddenly, Pongo had an idea. He made the puppies roll in some soot until they all looked like black Labradors.

Under the cover of their disguise, the puppies climbed into a van that was going to London. But falling snowflakes began to wash away the soot.

Cruella saw white patches appearing on the puppies' coats and realized that she had been tricked. "After them!" she shouted to the Baduns.

Pongo just had time to leap onto the bumper as the van sped off—with Cruella and the Baduns right behind.

Cruella was determined
to force the van off the road.
But as she banged into the side of
it, her car skidded out of control and
hurtled down a steep hill into
a snowdrift.

Then the Baduns' van crashed into
the back of Cruella's car—and they
all ended up in
a large pile of
wreckage!

Back in London and home at last, Roger, Anita, and Nanny hugged the tired puppies. Then Nanny said, "Have you noticed that there seems to be a lot more of them?"

Roger started to count. "Fourteen—sixty-two—ninety-four—and five over there. That's a hundred and one Dalmatians counting Perdita and Pongo!"

"Whatever are we going to do with them all?" asked Anita.

"Why, keep them of course," said Roger. "We'll buy a big house and have a Dalmatian Plantation!"

And that's exactly what they did!